A275

LORD WEARY'S CASTLE

LORD WEARY'S CASTLE

Robert Lowell

Harcourt, Brace & World, Inc. New York

To
JEAN

Some of these poems have appeared in *Partisan Review, The Sewanee Review, The Kenyon Review, The Nation, Common Sense, Portfolio, Foreground, The Commonweal, Poetry, The Virginia Quarterly,* and in "Land of Unlikeness," published by the Cummington Press.

Note

My title comes from an old ballad:

> "It's Lambkin was a mason good
> As ever built wi' stane:
> He built Lord Wearie's castle
> But payment gat he nane . . ."

When I use the word *after* below the title of a poem, what follows is not a translation but an imitation which should be read as though it were an original English poem. The last line of "The Shako" is taken literally from a translation by C. F. Mc-Intyre. "Our Lady of Walsingham" is an adaptation of several paragraphs from E. I. Watkin's *Catholic Art and Culture*. I hope that the source of "After the Surprising Conversions" will be recognized.

R. L.

Contents

ix

Suscipe, Domine, munera pro tuorum commemoratione Sanctorum: ut, sicut illos passio gloriosos effecit; ita nos devotio reddat innocuos.

The Exile's Return

THERE mounts in squalls a sort of rusty mire,
Not ice, not snow, to leaguer the Hôtel
De Ville, where braced pig-iron dragons grip
The blizzard to their rigor mortis. A bell
Grumbles when the reverberations strip
The thatching from its spire,
The search-guns click and spit and split up timber
And nick the slate roofs on the Holstenwall
Where torn-up tilestones crown the victor. Fall
And winter, spring and summer, guns unlimber
And lumber down the narrow gabled street
Past your gray, sorry and ancestral house
Where the dynamited walnut tree
Shadows a squat, old, wind-torn gate and cows
The Yankee commandant. You will not see
Strutting children or meet
The peg-leg and reproachful chancellor
With a forget-me-not in his button-hole
When the unseasoned liberators roll
Into the Market Square, ground arms before
The Rathaus; but already lily-stands
Burgeon the risen Rhineland, and a rough
Cathedral lifts its eye. Pleasant enough,
Voi ch'entrate, and your life is in your hands.

The Holy Innocents

LISTEN, the hay-bells tinkle as the cart
Wavers on rubber tires along the tar
And cindered ice below the burlap mill
And ale-wife run. The oxen drool and start
In wonder at the fenders of a car,
And blunder hugely up St. Peter's hill.
These are the undefiled by woman—their
Sorrow is not the sorrow of this world:
King Herod shrieking vengeance at the curled
Up knees of Jesus choking in the air,

A king of speechless clods and infants. Still
The world out-Herods Herod; and the year,
The nineteen-hundred forty-fifth of grace,
Lumbers with losses up the clinkered hill
Of our purgation; and the oxen near
The worn foundations of their resting-place,
The holy manger where their bed is corn
And holly torn for Christmas. If they die,
As Jesus, in the harness, who will mourn?
Lamb of the shepherds, Child, how still you lie.

Colloquy in Black Rock

Here the jack-hammer jabs into the ocean;
My heart, you race and stagger and demand
More blood-gangs for your nigger-brass percussions,
Till I, the stunned machine of your devotion,
Clanging upon this cymbal of a hand,
Am rattled screw and footloose. All discussions

End in the mud-flat detritus of death.
My heart, beat faster, faster. In Black Mud
Hungarian workmen give their blood
For the martyre Stephen, who was stoned to death.

Black Mud, a name to conjure with: O mud
For watermelons gutted to the crust,
Mud for the mole-tide harbor, mud for mouse,
Mud for the armored Diesel fishing tubs that thud
A year and a day to wind and tide; the dust
Is on this skipping heart that shakes my house,

House of our Savior who was hanged till death.
My heart, beat faster, faster. In Black Mud
Stephen the martyre was broken down to blood:
Our ransom is the rubble of his death.

Christ walks on the black water. In Black Mud
Darts the kingfisher. On Corpus Christi, heart,
Over the drum-beat of St. Stephen's choir
I hear him, *Stupor Mundi,* and the mud
Flies from his hunching wings and beak—my heart,
The blue kingfisher dives on you in fire.

Christmas in Black Rock

CHRIST God's red shadow hangs upon the wall
The dead leaf's echo on these hours
Whose burden spindles to no breath at all;
Hard at our heels the huntress moonlight towers
And the green needles bristle at the glass
Tiers of defense-plants where the treadmill night
Churns up Long Island Sound with piston-fist.
Tonight, my child, the lifeless leaves will mass,
Heaving and heaping, as the swivelled light
Burns on the bell-spar in the fruitless mist.

Christ Child, your lips are lean and evergreen
Tonight in Black Rock, and the moon
Sidles outside into the needle-screen
And strikes the hand that feeds you with a spoon
Tonight, as drunken Polish night-shifts walk
Over the causeway and their juke-box booms
Hosannah in excelsis Domino.
Tonight, my child, the foot-loose hallows stalk
Us down in the blind alleys of our rooms;
By the mined root the leaves will overflow.

December, old leech, has leafed through Autumn's store
Where Poland has unleashed its dogs
To bay the moon upon the Black Rock shore:
Under our windows, on the rotten logs
The moonbeam, bobbing like an apple, snags
The undertow. O Christ, the spiralling years
Slither with child and manger to a ball
Of ice; and what is man? We tear our rags
To hang the Furies by their itching ears,
And the green needles nail us to the wall.

New Year's Day

Again and then again . . . the year is born
To ice and death, and it will never do
To skulk behind storm-windows by the stove
To hear the postgirl sounding her French horn
When the thin tidal ice is wearing through.
Here is the understanding not to love
Our neighbor, or tomorrow that will sieve
Our resolutions. While we live, we live

To snuff the smoke of victims. In the snow
The kitten heaved its hindlegs, as if fouled,
And died. We bent it in a Christmas box
And scattered blazing weeds to scare the crow
Until the snake-tailed sea-winds coughed and howled
For alms outside the church whose double locks
Wait for St. Peter, the distorted key.
Under St. Peter's bell the parish sea

Swells with its smelt into the burlap shack
Where Joseph plucks his hand-lines like a harp,
And hears the fearful *Puer natus est*
Of Circumcision, and relives the wrack
And howls of Jesus whom he holds. How sharp
The burden of the Law before the beast:
Time and the grindstone and the knife of God.
The Child is born in blood, O child of blood.

The Quaker Graveyard in Nantucket

(FOR WARREN WINSLOW, DEAD AT SEA)

Let man have dominion over the fishes of the sea and the fowls of the air and the beasts and the whole earth, and every creeping creature that moveth upon the earth.

I

A BRACKISH reach of shoal off Madaket,—
The sea was still breaking violently and night
Had steamed into our North Atlantic Fleet,
When the drowned sailor clutched the drag-net. Light
Flashed from his matted head and marble feet,
He grappled at the net
With the coiled, hurdling muscles of his thighs:
The corpse was bloodless, a botch of reds and whites,
Its open, staring eyes
Were lustreless dead-lights
Or cabin-windows on a stranded hulk
Heavy with sand. We weight the body, close
Its eyes and heave it seaward whence it came,
Where the heel-headed dogfish barks its nose
On Ahab's void and forehead; and the name
Is blocked in yellow chalk.
Sailors, who pitch this portent at the sea
Where dreadnaughts shall confess
Its hell-bent deity,
When you are powerless
To sand-bag this Atlantic bulwark, faced
By the earth-shaker, green, unwearied, chaste
In his steel scales: ask for no Orphean lute
To pluck life back. The guns of the steeled fleet
Recoil and then repeat
The hoarse salute.

II

Whenever winds are moving and their breath
Heaves at the roped-in bulwarks of this pier,
The terns and sea-gulls tremble at your death
In these home waters. Sailor, can you hear
The Pequod's sea wings, beating landward, fall
Headlong and break on our Atlantic wall
Off 'Sconset, where the yawing S-boats splash
The bellbuoy, with ballooning spinnakers,
As the entangled, screeching mainsheet clears
The blocks: off Madaket, where lubbers lash
The heavy surf and throw their long lead squids
For blue-fish? Sea-gulls blink their heavy lids
Seaward. The winds' wings beat upon the stones,
Cousin, and scream for you and the claws rush
At the sea's throat and wring it in the slush
Of this old Quaker graveyard where the bones
Cry out in the long night for the hurt beast
Bobbing by Ahab's whaleboats in the East.

III

All you recovered from Poseidon died
With you, my cousin, and the harrowed brine
Is fruitless on the blue beard of the god,
Stretching beyond us to the castles in Spain,
Nantucket's westward haven. To Cape Cod
Guns, cradled on the tide,
Blast the eelgrass about a waterclock
Of bilge and backwash, roil the salt and sand
Lashing earth's scaffold, rock
Our warships in the hand
Of the great God, where time's contrition blues
Whatever it was these Quaker sailors lost
In the mad scramble of their lives. They died
When time was open-eyed,
Wooden and childish; only bones abide
There, in the nowhere, where their boats were tossed
Sky-high, where mariners had fabled news
Of IS, the whited monster. What it cost
Them is their secret. In the sperm-whale's slick
I see the Quakers drown and hear their cry:
"If God himself had not been on our side,
If God himself had not been on our side,
When the Atlantic rose against us, why,
Then it had swallowed us up quick."

IV

This is the end of the whaleroad and the whale *[kenning]*
Who spewed Nantucket bones on the thrashed swell
And stirred the troubled waters to whirlpools
To send the Pequod packing off to hell:
This is the end of them, three-quarters fools,
Snatching at straws to sail
Seaward and seaward on the turntail whale,
Spouting out blood and water as it rolls,
Sick as a dog to these Atlantic shoals:
Clamavimus, O depths. Let the sea-gulls wail

For water, for the deep where the high tide
Mutters to its hurt self, mutters and ebbs.
Waves wallow in their wash, go out and out,
Leave only the death-rattle of the crabs,
The beach increasing, its enormous snout
Sucking the ocean's side.
This is the end of running on the waves;
We are poured out like water. Who will dance
The mast-lashed master of Leviathans
Up from this field of Quakers in their unstoned graves?

V

WHEN the whale's viscera go and the roll
Of its corruption overruns this world
Beyond tree-swept Nantucket and Wood's Hole
And Martha's Vineyard, Sailor, will your sword
Whistle and fall and sink into the fat?
In the great ash-pit of Jehoshaphat
The bones cry for the blood of the white whale,
The fat flukes arch and whack about its ears,
The death-lance churns into the sanctuary, tears
The gun-blue swingle, heaving like a flail,
And hacks the coiling life out: it works and drags
And rips the sperm-whale's midriff into rags,
Gobbets of blubber spill to wind and weather,
Sailor, and gulls go round the stoven timbers
Where the morning stars sing out together
And thunder shakes the white surf and dismembers
The red flag hammered in the mast-head. Hide,
Our steel, Jonas Messias, in Thy side.

OUR LADY OF WALSINGHAM

THERE once the penitents took off their shoes
And then walked barefoot the remaining mile;
And the small trees, a stream and hedgerows file
Slowly along the munching English lane,
Like cows to the old shrine, until you lose
Track of your dragging pain.
The stream flows down under the druid tree,
Shiloah's whirlpools gurgle and make glad
The castle of God. Sailor, you were glad
And whistled Sion by that stream. But see:

Our Lady, too small for her canopy,
Sits near the altar. There's no comeliness
At all or charm in that expressionless
Face with its heavy eyelids. As before,
This face, for centuries a memory,
Non est species, neque decor,
Expressionless, expresses God: it goes
Past castled Sion. She knows what God knows,
Not Calvary's Cross nor crib at Bethlehem
Now, and the world shall come to Walsingham.

THE EMPTY winds are creaking and the oak
Splatters and splatters on the cenotaph,
The boughs are trembling and a gaff
Bobs on the untimely stroke
Of the greased wash exploding on a shoal-bell
In the old mouth of the Atlantic. It's well;
Atlantic, you are fouled with the blue sailors,
Sea-monsters, upward angel, downward fish:
Unmarried and corroding, spare of flesh
Mart once of supercilious, wing'd clippers,
Atlantic, where your bell-trap guts its spoil
You could cut the brackish winds with a knife
Here in Nantucket, and cast up the time
When the Lord God formed man from the sea's slime
And breathed into his face the breath of life,
And blue-lung'd combers lumbered to the kill.
The Lord survives the rainbow of His will.

The First Sunday in Lent

IN THE ATTIC

THE CROOKED family chestnut sighs, for March,
Time's fool, is storming up and down the town;
The gray snow squelches and the well-born stamp
From sermons in a scolded, sober mob
That wears away the Sabbath with a frown,
A world below my window. What will clamp
The weak-kneed roots together when the damp
Aches like a conscience, and they grope to rob
The hero under his triumphal arch?

This is the fifth floor attic where I hid
My stolen agates and the cannister
Preserved from Bunker Hill—feathers and guns,
Matchlock and flintlock and percussion-cap;
Gettysburg etched upon the cylinder
Of Father's Colt. A Lüger of a Hun,
Once blue as Satan, breaks Napoleon,
My china pitcher. Cartridge boxes trap
A chipmunk on the saber where they slid.

On Troy's last day, alas, the populous
Shrines held carnival, and girls and boys
Flung garlands to the wooden horse; so we
Burrow into the lion's mouth to die.
Lord, from the lust and dust thy will destroys
Raise an unblemished Adam who will see
The limbs of the tormented chestnut tree
Tingle, and hear the March-winds lift and cry:
"The Lord of Hosts will overshadow us."

15

THE FERRIS WHEEL

THIS world, this ferris wheel, is tired and strains
Its townsman's humorous and bulging eye,
As he ascends and lurches from his seat
And dangles by a shoe-string overhead
To tell the racing world that it must die.
Who can remember what his father said?
The little wheel is turning on the great
In the white water of Christ's blood. The red
Eagle of Ares swings along the lanes,

Of camp-stools where the many watch the sky:
The townsman hangs, the eagle swings. It stoops
And lifts the ferris wheel into the tent
Pitched for the devil. But the man works loose,
He drags and zigzags through the circus hoops,
And lion-taming Satan bows and loops
His cracking tail into a hangman's noose;
He is the only happy man in Lent.
He laughs into my face until I cry.

Christmas Eve Under Hooker's Statue

TONIGHT a blackout. Twenty years ago
I hung my stocking on the tree, and hell's
Serpent entwined the apple in the toe
To sting the child with knowledge. Hooker's heels
Kicking at nothing in the shifting snow,
A cannon and a cairn of cannon balls
Rusting before the blackened Statehouse, know
How the long horn of plenty broke like glass
In Hooker's gauntlets. Once I came from Mass;

Now storm-clouds shelter Christmas, once again
Mars meets his fruitless star with open arms,
His heavy saber flashes with the rime,
The war-god's bronzed and empty forehead forms
Anonymous machinery from raw men;
The cannon on the Common cannot stun
The blundering butcher as he rides on Time—
The barrel clinks with holly. I am cold:
I ask for bread, my father gives me mould;

His stocking is full of stones. Santa in red
Is crowned with wizened berries. Man of war,
Where is the summer's garden? In its bed
The ancient speckled serpent will appear,
And black-eyed susan with her frizzled head.
When Chancellorsville mowed down the volunteer,
"All wars are boyish," Herman Melville said;
But we are old, our fields are running wild:
Till Christ again turn wanderer and child.

Buttercups

When we were children our papas were stout
And colorless as seaweed or the floats
At anchor off New Bedford. We were shut
In gardens where our brassy sailor coats
Made us like black-eyed susans bending out
Into the ocean. Then my teeth were cut:
A levelled broom-pole butt
Was pushed into my thin
And up-turned chin—
There were shod hoofs behind the horseplay. But
I played Napoleon in my attic cell
Until my shouldered broom
Bobbed down the room
With horse and neighing shell.

Recall the shadows the doll-curtains veined
On Ancrem Winslow's ponderous plate from blue
China, the breaking of time's haggard tide
On the huge cobwebbed print of Waterloo,
With a cracked smile across the glass. I cried
To see the Emperor's sabered eagle slide
From the clutching grenadier
Staff-officer
With the gold leaf cascading down his side—
A red dragoon, his plough-horse rearing, swayed
Back on his reins to crop
The buttercup
Bursting upon the braid.

In Memory of Arthur Winslow

DEATH FROM CANCER

This Easter, Arthur Winslow, less than dead,
Your people set you up in Phillips' House
To settle off your wrestling with the crab—
The claws drop flesh upon your yachting blouse
Until longshoreman Charon come and stab
Through your adjusted bed
And crush the crab. On Boston Basin, shells
Hit water by the Union Boat Club wharf:
You ponder why the coxes' squeakings dwarf
The *resurrexit dominus* of all the bells.

Grandfather Winslow, look, the swanboats coast
That island in the Public Gardens, where
The bread-stuffed ducks are brooding, where with tub
And strainer the mid-Sunday Irish scare
The sun-struck shallows for the dusky chub
This Easter, and the ghost
Of risen Jesus walks the waves to run
Arthur upon a trumpeting black swan
Beyond Charles River to the Acheron
Where the wide waters and their voyager are one.

DUNBARTON

THE STONES are yellow and the grass is gray
Past Concord by the rotten lake and hill
Where crutch and trumpet meet the limousine
And half-forgotten Starks and Winslows fill
The granite plot and the dwarf pines are green
From watching for the day
When the great year of the little yeomen come
Bringing its landed Promise and the faith
That made the Pilgrim Makers take a lathe
And point their wooden steeples lest the Word be dumb.

O fearful witnesses, your day is done:
The minister from Boston waves your shades,
Like children, out of sight and out of mind.
The first selectman of Dunbarton spreads
Wreaths of New Hampshire pine cones on the lined
Casket where the cold sun
Is melting. But, at last, the end is reached;
We start our cars. The preacher's mouthings still
Deafen my poor relations on the hill:
Their sunken landmarks echo what our fathers preached.

FIVE YEARS LATER

THIS Easter, Arthur Winslow, five years gone
I came to mourn you, not to praise the craft
That netted you a million dollars, late
Hosing out gold in Colorado's waste,
Then lost it all in Boston real estate.
Now from the train, at dawn
Leaving Columbus in Ohio, shell
On shell of our stark culture strikes the sun
To fill my head with all our fathers won
When Cotton Mather wrestled with the fiends from hell.

You must have hankered for our family's craft:
The block-house Edward made, the Governor,
At Marshfield, and the slight coin-silver spoons
The Sheriff beat to shame the gaunt Revere,
And General Stark's coarse bas-relief in bronze
Set on your granite shaft
In rough Dunbarton; for what else could bring
You, Arthur, to the veined and alien West
But devil's notions that your gold at least
Could give back life to men who whipped or backed the King?

IV

A PRAYER FOR MY GRANDFATHER TO OUR LADY

Mother, for these three hundred years or more
Neither our clippers nor our slavers reached
The haven of your peace in this Bay State:
Neither my father nor his father. Beached
On these dry flats of fishy real estate,
O Mother, I implore
Your scorched, blue thunderbreasts of love to pour
Buckets of blessings on my burning head
Until I rise like Lazarus from the dead:
Lavabis nos et super nivem dealbabor.

"On Copley Square, I saw you hold the door
To Trinity, the costly Church, and saw
The painted Paradise of harps and lutes
Sink like Atlantis in the Devil's jaw
And knock the Devil's teeth out by the roots;
But when I strike for shore
I find no painted idols to adore:
Hell is burned out, heaven's harp-strings are slack.
Mother, run to the chalice, and bring back
Blood on your finger-tips for Lazarus who was poor."

Winter in Dunbarton

Time smiling on this sundial of a world
Sweltered about the snowman and the worm,
Sacker of painted idols and the peers
Of Europe; but my cat is cold, is curled
Tight as a boulder: she no longer smears
Her catnip mouse from Christmas, for the germ—
Mindless and ice, a world against our world—
Has tamped her round of brains into her ears.

This winter all the snowmen turn to stone,
Or, sick of the long hurly-burly, rise
Like butterflies into Jehovah's eyes
And shift until their crystals must atone

In water. Belle, the cat that used to rat
About my father's books, is dead. All day
The wastes of snow about my house stare in
Through idle windows at the brainless cat;
The coke-barrel in the corner whimpers. May
The snow recede and red clay furrows set
In the grim grin of their erosion, in
The caterpillar tents and roadslides, fat

With muck and winter dropsy, where the tall
Snow-monster wipes the coke-fumes from his eyes
And scatters his corruption and it lies
Gaping until the fungus-eyeballs fall

Into this eldest of the seasons. Cold
Snaps the bronze toes and fingers of the Christ
My father fetched from Florence, and the dead
Chatters to nothing in the thankless ground
His father screwed from Charlie Stark and sold
To the selectmen. Cold has cramped his head
Against his heart: my father's stone is crowned
With snowflakes and the bronze-age shards of Christ.

Mary Winslow

Her irish maids could never spoon out mush
Or orange-juice enough; the body cools
And smiles as a sick child
Who adds up figures, and a hush
Grips at the poised relations sipping sherry
And tracking up the carpets of her four
Room kingdom. On the rigid Charles, in snow,
Charon, the Lubber, clambers from his wherry,
And stops her hideous baby-squawks and yells,
Wit's clownish afterthought. Nothing will go
Again. Even the gelded picador
Baiting the twinned runt bulls
With walrus horns before the Spanish Belles
Is veiled with all the childish bibelots.

Mary Winslow is dead. Out on the Charles
The shells hold water and their oarblades drag,
Littered with captivated ducks, and now
The bell-rope in King's Chapel Tower unsnarls
And bells the bestial cow
From Boston Common; she is dead. But stop,
Neighbor, these pillows prop
Her that her terrified and child's cold eyes
Glass what they're not: our Copley ancestress,
Grandiloquent, square-jowled and worldly-wise,
A Cleopatra in her housewife's dress;
Nothing will go again. The bells cry: "Come,
Come home," the babbling Chapel belfry cries:
"Come, Mary Winslow, come; I bell thee home."

Salem

In salem seasick spindrift drifts or skips
To the canvas flapping on the seaward panes
Until the knitting sailor stabs at ships
Nosing like sheep of Morpheus through his brain's
Asylum. Seaman, seaman, how the draft
Lashes the oily slick about your head,
Beating up whitecaps! Seaman, Charon's raft
Dumps its damned goods into the harbor-bed,—
There sewage sickens the rebellious seas.
Remember, seaman, Salem fishermen
Once hung their nimble fleets on the Great Banks.
Where was it that New England bred the men
Who quartered the Leviathan's fat flanks
And fought the British Lion to his knees?

Concord

TEN THOUSAND Fords are idle here in search
Of a tradition. Over these dry sticks—
The Minute Man, the Irish Catholics,
The ruined bridge and Walden's fished-out perch—
The belfry of the Unitarian Church
Rings out the hanging Jesus. Crucifix,
How can your whited spindling arms transfix
Mammon's unbridled industry, the lurch
For forms to harness Heraclitus' stream!
This Church is Concord—Concord where Thoreau
Named all the birds without a gun to probe
Through darkness to the painted man and bow:
The death-dance of King Philip and his scream
Whose echo girdled this imperfect globe.

Children of Light

Our FATHERS wrung their bread from stocks and stones
And fenced their gardens with the Redman's bones;
Embarking from the Nether Land of Holland,
Pilgrims unhouseled by Geneva's night,
They planted here the Serpent's seeds of light;
And here the pivoting searchlights probe to shock
The riotous glass houses built on rock,
And candles gutter by an empty altar,
And light is where the landless blood of Cain
Is burning, burning the unburied grain.

Rebellion

THERE was rebellion, father, when the mock
French windows slammed and you hove backward, rammed
Into your heirlooms, screens, a glass-cased clock,
The highboy quaking to its toes. You damned
My arm that cast your house upon your head
And broke the chimney flintlock on your skull.
Last night the moon was full:
I dreamed the dead
Caught at my knees and fell:
And it was well
With me, my father. Then
Behemoth and Leviathan
Devoured our mighty merchants. None could arm
Or put to sea. O father, on my farm
I added field to field
And I have sealed
An everlasting pact
With Dives to contract
The world that spreads in pain;
But the world spread
When the clubbed flintlock broke my father's brain.

At a Bible House

At a Bible House
Where smoking is forbidden
By the Prophet's law,
I saw you wiry, bed-ridden,
Gone in the kidneys; raw
Onions and a louse
Twitched on the sheet before
The palsy of your white
Stubble—a Mennonite
Or die-hard Doukabor,
God-rooted, hard. You spoke
Whistling gristle-words
Half inaudible
To us: of raw-boned birds
Migrating from the smoke
Of cities, of a gull
Perched on the redwood
Thrusting short awl-shaped leaves:
Three hundred feet of love
Where the Pacific heaves
The tap-root—wise above
Man's wisdom with the food
Squeezed from three thousand years'
Standing. It is all
A moment. The trees
Grow earthward: neither good
Nor evil, hopes nor fears,
Repulsion nor desire,
Earth, water, air or fire
Will serve to stay the fall.

The Drunken Fisherman

Wallowing in this bloody sty,
I cast for fish that pleased my eye
(Truly Jehovah's bow suspends
No pots of gold to weight its ends);
Only the blood-mouthed rainbow trout
Rose to my bait. They flopped about
My canvas creel until the moth
Corrupted its unstable cloth.

A calendar to tell the day;
A handkerchief to wave away
The gnats; a couch unstuffed with storm
Pouching a bottle in one arm;
A whiskey bottle full of worms;
And bedroom slacks: are these fit terms
To mete the worm whose molten rage
Boils in the belly of old age?

Once fishing was a rabbit's foot—
O wind blow cold, O wind blow hot,
Let suns stay in or suns step out:
Life danced a jig on the sperm-whale's spout—
The fisher's fluent and obscene
Catches kept his conscience clean.
Children, the raging memory drools
Over the glory of past pools.

Now the hot river, ebbing, hauls
Its bloody waters into holes;
A grain of sand inside my shoe
Mimics the moon that might undo
Man and Creation too; remorse,
Stinking, has puddled up its source;
Here tantrums thrash to a whale's rage.
This is the pot-hole of old age.

Is there no way to cast my hook
Out of this dynamited brook?
The Fisher's sons must cast about
When shallow waters peter out.
I will catch Christ with a greased worm,
And when the Prince of Darkness stalks
My bloodstream to its Stygian term . . .
On water the Man-Fisher walks.

The North Sea Undertaker's Complaint

Now SOUTH and south and south the mallard heads,
His green-blue bony hood echoes the green
Flats of the Weser, and the mussel beds
Are sluggish where the webbed feet spanked the lean
Eel grass to tinder in the take-off. South
Is what I think of. It seems yesterday
I slid my hearse across the river mouth
And pitched the first iced mouse into the hay.
Thirty below it is. I hear our dumb
Club-footed orphan ring the Angelus
And clank the bell-chain for St. Gertrude's choir
To wail with the dead bell the martyrdom
Of one more blue-lipped priest; the phosphorous
Melted the hammer of his heart to fire.

Napoleon Crosses the Berezina

"There will the eagles be gathered together"

HERE Charlemagne's stunted shadow plays charades
With pawns and bishops whose play-cannister
Shivers the Snowman's bones, and the Great Bear
Shuffles away to his ancestral shades,
For here Napoleon Bonaparte parades;
Hussar and cuirassier and grenadier
Ascend the tombstone steppes to Russia. Here
The eagles gather as the West invades
The Holy Land of Russia. Lord and glory
Of dragonish, unfathomed waters, rise!
Although your Berezina cannot gnaw
These soldier-plumed pontoons to matchwood, ice
Is tuning them to tumbrils, and the snow
Blazes its carrion-miles to Purgatory.

The Soldier

In time of war you could not save your skin.
Where is that Ghibelline whom Dante met
On Purgatory's doorstep, without kin
To set up chantries for his God-held debt?
So far from Campaldino, no one knows
Where he is buried by the Archiano
Whose source is Camaldoli, through the snows,
Fuggendo a piedi e sanguinando il piano,
The soldier drowned face downward in his blood.
Until the thaw he waited, then the flood
Roared like a wounded dragon over shoal
And reef and snatched away his crucifix
And rolled his body like a log to Styx;
Two angels fought with bill-hooks for his soul.

War

(AFTER RIMBAUD)

Where basilisk and mortar lob their lead
Whistling against the cloud sheep overhead,
Scarlet or green, before their black-tongued Sire,
The massed battalions flounder into fire
Until the furnace of affliction turns
A hundred thousand men to stone and burns
The poor dead in the summer grass. Their friend,
The earth, was low and thrifty to this end:
It is a god untouched by papal bulls,
The great gold chalice and the thuribles:
Cradled on its hosannahs, it will rock,
Dead to the world, until their mother, fat
With weeping underneath her cracked black hat,
Hands it her penny knotted in a sock.

Charles the Fifth and the Peasant

(AFTER VALÉRY)

Elected Kaiser, burgher and a knight,
Clamped in his black and burly harness, Charles
Canters on Titian's sunset to his night;
A wounded wolfhound bites his spurs and snarls:
So middle-aged and common, it's absurd
To picture him as Caesar, the first cause
Behind whose leg-of-mutton beard, the jaws
Grate on the flesh and gristle of the Word.

The fir trees in the background buzz and lurch
To the disgruntled sing-song of their fears:
"How can we stop it, stop it, stop it?" sing
The needles; and the peasant, braining perch
Against a bucket, rocks and never hears
His Ark drown in the deluge of the King.

The Shako

(AFTER RILKE)

Night and its muffled creakings, as the wheels
Of Blücher's caissons circle with the clock;
He lifts his eyes and drums until he feels
The clavier shudder and allows the rock
And Scylla of her eyes to fix his face:
It is as though he looks into a glass
Reflecting on this guilty breathing-space
His terror and the salvos of the brass
From Brandenburg. She moves away. Instead,
Wearily by the broken altar, Abel
Remembers how the brothers fell apart
And hears the friendless hacking of his heart,
And strangely foreign on the mirror-table
Leans the black shako with its white death's-head.

France

My HUMAN brothers who live after me,
See how I hang. My bones eat through the skin
And flesh they carried here upon the chin
And lipping clutch of their cupidity;
Now here, now there, the starling and the sea
Gull splinter the groined eyeballs of my sin,
Brothers, more beaks of birds than needles in
The fathoms of the Bayeux Tapestry:
"God wills it, wills it, wills it: it is blood."
My brothers, if I call you brothers, see:
The blood of Abel crying from the dead
Sticks to my blackened skull and eyes. What good
Are *lebensraum* and bread to Abel dead
And rotten on the cross-beams of the tree?

1790

(FROM THE MEMOIRS OF GENERAL THIEBAULT)

ON MAUNDY THURSDAY when the King and Queen
Had washed and wiped the chosen poor and fed
Them from a boisterous wooden platter; here
We stood in forage-caps upon the green:
Green guardsmen of the Nation and its head.
The King walked out into the biting air,
Two gentlemen went with him; as they neared
Our middle gate, we stood aside for welcome;
A stone's throw lay between us when they cleared
Two horse-shoe flights of steps and crossed the Place Vendome.

"What a dog's life it is to be a king,"
I grumbled and unslung my gun; the chaff
And cinders whipped me and began to sting.
I heard our Monarch's Breughel-peasant laugh
Exploding, as a spaniel mucked with tar
Cut by his Highness' ankles on the double-quick
To fetch its stamping mistress. Louis smashed
Its backbone with a backstroke of his stick:
Slouching a little more than usual, he splashed
As boyish as a stallion to the Champs de Mars.

Between the Porch and the Altar

MOTHER AND SON

MEETING his mother makes him lose ten years,
Or is it twenty? Time, no doubt, has ears
That listen to the swallowed serpent, wound
Into its bowels, but he thinks no sound
Is possible before her, he thinks the past
Is settled. It is honest to hold fast
Merely to what one sees with one's own eyes
When the red velvet curves and haunches rise
To blot him from the pretty driftwood fire's
Façade of welcome. Then the son retires
Into the sack and selfhood of the boy
Who clawed through fallen houses of his Troy,
Homely and human only when the flames
Crackle in recollection. Nothing shames
Him more than this uncoiling, counterfeit
Body presented as an idol. It
Is something in a circus, big as life,
The painted dragon, a mother and a wife
With flat glass eyes pushed at him on a stick;
The human mover crawls to make them click.
The forehead of her father's portrait peels
With rosy dryness, and the schoolboy kneels
To ask the benediction of the hand,
Lifted as though to motion him to stand,
Dangling its watch-chain on the Holy Book—
A little golden snake that mouths a hook.

ADAM AND EVE

THE FARMER sizzles on his shaft all day.
He is content and centuries away
From white-hot Concord, and he stands on guard.
Or is he melting down like sculptured lard?
His hand is crisp and steady on the plough.
I quarrelled with you, but am happy now
To while away my life for your unrest
Of terror. Never to have lived is best;
Man tasted Eve with death. I taste my wife
And children while I hold your hands. I knife
Their names into this elm. What is exempt?
I eye the statue with an awed contempt
And see the puritanical façade
Of the white church that Irish exiles made
For Patrick—that Colonial from Rome
Had magicked the charmed serpents from their home,
As though he were the Piper. Will his breath
Scorch the red dragon of my nerves to death?
By sundown we are on a shore. You walk
A little way before me and I talk,
Half to myself and half aloud. They lied,
My cold-eyed seedy fathers when they died,
Or rather threw their lives away, to fix
Sterile, forbidding nameplates on the bricks
Above a kettle. Jesus rest their souls!
You cry for help. Your market-basket rolls
With all its baking apples in the lake.
You watch the whorish slither of a snake
That chokes a duckling. When we try to kiss,
Our eyes are slits and cringing, and we hiss;
Scales glitter on our bodies as we fall.
The Farmer melts upon his pedestal.

KATHERINE'S DREAM

It must have been a Friday. I could hear
The top-floor typist's thunder and the beer
That you had brought in cases hurt my head;
I'd sent the pillows flying from my bed,
I hugged my knees together and I gasped.
The dangling telephone receiver rasped
Like someone in a dream who cannot stop
For breath or logic till his victim drop
To darkness and the sheets. I must have slept,
But still could hear my father who had kept
Your guilty presents but cut off my hair.
He whispers that he really doesn't care
If I am your kept woman all my life,
Or ruin your two children and your wife;
But my dishonor makes him drink. Of course
I'll tell the court the truth for his divorce.
I walk through snow into St. Patrick's yard.
Black nuns with glasses smile and stand on guard
Before a bulkhead in a bank of snow,
Whose charred doors open, as good people go
Inside by twos to the confessor. One
Must have a friend to enter there, but none
Is friendless in this crowd, and the nuns smile.
I stand aside and marvel; for a while
The winter sun is pleasant and it warms
My heart with love for others, but the swarms
Of penitents have dwindled. I begin
To cry and ask God's pardon of our sin.

Where are you? You were with me and are gone.
All the forgiven couples hurry on
To dinner and their nights, and none will stop.
I run about in circles till I drop
Against a padlocked bulkhead in a yard
Where faces redden and the snow is hard.

AT THE ALTAR

I sit at a gold table with my girl
Whose eyelids burn with brandy. What a whirl
Of Easter eggs is colored by the lights,
As the Norwegian dancer's crystalled tights
Flash with her naked leg's high-booted skate,
Like Northern Lights upon my watching plate.
The twinkling steel above me is a star;
I am a fallen Christmas tree. Our car
Races through seven red-lights—then the road
Is unpatrolled and empty, and a load
Of ply-wood with a tail-light makes us slow.
I turn and whisper in her ear. You know
I want to leave my mother and my wife,
You wouldn't have me tied to them for life . . .
Time runs, the windshield runs with stars. The past
Is cities from a train, until at last
Its escalating and black-windowed blocks
Recoil against a Gothic church. The clocks
Are tolling. I am dying. The shocked stones
Are falling like a ton of bricks and bones
That snap and splinter and descend in glass
Before a priest who mumbles through his Mass
And sprinkles holy water; and the Day
Breaks with its lightning on the man of clay,
Dies amara valde. Here the Lord
Is Lucifer in harness: hand on sword,
He watches me for Mother, and will turn
The bier and baby-carriage where I burn.

To Peter Taylor on the Feast of the Epiphany

Peter, the war has taught me to revere
The rulers of this darkness, for I fear
That only Armageddon will suffice
To turn the hero skating on thin ice
When Whore and Beast and Dragon rise for air
From allegoric waters. Fear is where
We hunger: where the Irishmen recall
How wisdom trailed a star into a stall
And knelt in sacred terror to confer
Its fabulous gold and frankincense and myrrh:
And where the lantern-noses scrimmage down
The highway to the sea below this town
And the sharp barker rigs his pre-war planes
To lift old Adam's dollars for his pains;
There on the thawing ice, in red and white
And blue, the bugs are buzzing for the flight.
December's daylight hours have gone their round
Of sorrows with the sun into the sound,
And still the grandsires battle through the slush
To storm the landing biplanes with a rush—
Until their cash and somersaulting snare
Fear with its fingered stop-watch in mid-air.

As a Plane Tree by the Water

Darkness has called to darkness, and disgrace
Elbows about our windows in this planned
Babel of Boston where our money talks
And multiplies the darkness of a land
Of preparation where the Virgin walks
And roses spiral her enamelled face
Or fall to splinters on unwatered streets.
Our Lady of Babylon, go by, go by,
I was once the apple of your eye;
Flies, flies are on the plane tree, on the streets.

The flies, the flies, the flies of Babylon
Buzz in my ear-drums while the devil's long
Dirge of the people detonates the hour
For floating cities where his golden tongue
Enchants the masons of the Babel Tower
To raise tomorrow's city to the sun
That never sets upon these hell-fire streets
Of Boston, where the sunlight is a sword
Striking at the withholder of the Lord:
Flies, flies are on the plane tree, on the streets.

Flies strike the miraculous waters of the iced
Atlantic and the eyes of Bernadette
Who saw Our Lady standing in the cave
At Massabielle, saw her so squarely that
Her vision put out reason's eyes. The grave
Is open-mouthed and swallowed up in Christ.
O walls of Jericho! And all the streets
To our Atlantic wall are singing: "Sing,
Sing for the resurrection of the King."
Flies, flies are on the plane tree, on the streets.

The Crucifix

How DRY time screaks in its fat axle-grease,
As spare November strikes us through the ice
And the Leviathan breaks water in the rice
Fields, at the poles, at the hot gates to Greece;
It's time: the old unmastered lion roars
And ramps like a mad dog outside the doors,
Snapping at gobbets in my thumbless hand.
The seaways lurch through Sodom's knees of sand
Tomorrow. We are sinking. "Run, rat, run,"
The prophets thunder, and I run upon
My father, Adam. Adam, if our land
Become the desolation of a hand
That shakes the Temple back to clay, how can
War ever change my old into new man?
Get out from under my feet, old man. Let me pass;
On Ninth Street, through the Hallowe'en's soaped glass,
I picked at an old bone on two crossed sticks
And found, to *Via et Vita et Veritas*
A stray dog's signpost is a crucifix.

48

Dea Roma

AUGUSTUS mended you. He hung the tongue
Of Tullius upon your rostrum, lashed
The money-lenders from your Senate-house;
And Brutus bled his forty-six per cent
For *Pax Romana*. Quiet as a mouse
Blood licks the king's cosmetics with its tongue.

Some years, your legions soldiered through this world
Under the eagles of Lord Lucifer;
But human torches lit the captains home
Where victims warped the royal crucifix:
How many roads and sewers led to Rome.
Satan is pacing up and down the world

These sixteen centuries, Eternal City,
That we have squandered since Maxentius fell
Under the Milvian Bridge; from the dry dome
Of Michelangelo, your fisherman
Walks on the waters of a draining Rome
To bank his catch in the Celestial City.

The Ghost

(AFTER SEXTUS PROPERTIUS)

A GHOST is someone: death has left a hole
For the lead-colored soul to beat the fire:
 Cynthia leaves her dirty pyre
 And seems to coil herself and roll
  Under my canopy,
Love's stale and public playground, where I lie
And fill the run-down empire of my bed.
I see the street, her potter's field, is red
And lively with the ashes of the dead;

But she no longer sparkles off in smoke:
It is the body carted to the gate
 Last Friday, when the sizzling grate
 Left its charred furrows on her smock
  And ate into her hip.
A black nail dangles from a finger-tip
And Lethe oozes from her nether lip.
Her thumb-bones rattle on her brittle hands,
As Cynthia stamps and hisses and demands:

"Sextus, has sleep already washed away
Your manhood? You forget the window-sill
 My sliding wore to slivers? Day
 Would break before the Seven Hills
  Saw Cynthia retreat
And climb your shoulders to the knotted sheet.
You shouldered me and galloped on bare feet
To lay me by the crossroads. Have no fear:
Notus, who snatched your promise, has no ear.

50

"But why did no one call in my deaf ear?
Your calling would have gained me one more day.
　　Sextus, although you ran away
　　You might have called and stopped my bier
　　　A second by your door.
No tears drenched a black toga for your whore
When broken tilestones bruised her face before
The Capitol. Would it have strained your purse
To scatter ten cheap roses on my hearse?

"The State will make Pompilia's Chloris burn:
I knew her secret when I kissed the skull
　　Of Pluto in the tainted bowl.
　　Let Nomas burn her books and turn
　　　Her poisons into gold;
The finger-prints upon the potsherd told
Her love. You let a slut, whose body sold
To Thracians, liquefy my golden bust
In the coarse flame that crinkled me to dust.

"If Chloris' bed has left you with your head,
Lover, I think you'll answer my arrears:
　　My nurse is getting on in years,
　　See that she gets a little bread—
　　　She never clutched your purse;
See that my little humpback hears no curse
From her close-fisted friend. But burn. the verse
You bellowed half a lifetime in my name:
Why should you feed me to the fires of fame?

"I will not hound you, much as you have earned
It, Sextus: I shall reign in your four books—
  I swear this by the Hag who looks
  Into my heart where it was burned:
    Propertius, I kept faith;
If not, may serpents suck my ghost to death
And spit it with their forked and killing breath
Into the Styx where Agamemnon's wife
Founders in the green circles of her life.

"Beat the sycophant ivy from my urn,
That twists its binding shoots about my bones
  Where apple-sweetened Anio drones
  Through orchards that will never burn
    While honest Herakles,
My patron, watches. Anio, you will please
Me if you whisper upon sliding knees:
'Propertius, Cynthia is here:
She shakes her blossoms when my waters clear.'

"You cannot turn your back upon a dream,
For phantoms have their reasons when they come:
  We wander midnights: then the numb
  Ghost wades from the Lethean stream;
    Even the foolish dog
Stops its hell-raising mouths and casts its clog;
At cock-crow Charon checks us in his log.
Others can have you, Sextus; I alone
Hold: and I grind your manhood bone on bone."

In the Cage

THE LIFERS file into the hall,
According to their houses—twos
Of laundered denim. On the wall
A colored fairy tinkles blues
And titters by the balustrade;
Canaries beat their bars and scream.
We come from tunnels where the spade
Pick-axe and hod for plaster steam
In mud and insulation. Here
The Bible-twisting Israelite
Fasts for his Harlem. It is night,
And it is vanity, and age
Blackens the heart of Adam. Fear,
The yellow chirper, beaks its cage.

At the Indian Killer's Grave

"Here, also, are the veterans of King Philip's War,
who burned villages and slaughtered young and old,
with pious fierceness, while the godly souls through-
out the land were helping them with prayer."

BEHIND King's Chapel what the earth has kept
Whole from the jerking noose of time extends
Its dark enigma to Jehoshaphat;
Or will King Philip plait
The just man's scalp in the wailing valley! Friends,
Blacker than these black stones the subway bends
About the dirty elm roots and the well
For the unchristened infants in the waste
Of the great garden rotten to its root;
Death, the engraver, puts forward his bone foot
And Grace-with-wings and Time-on-wings compel
All this antique abandon of the disgraced
To face Jehovah's buffets and his ends.

The dusty leaves and frizzled lilacs gear
This garden of the elders with baroque
And prodigal embellishments but smoke,
Settling upon the pilgrims and their grounds,
Espouses and confounds
Their dust with the off-scourings of the town;
The libertarian crown
Of England built their mausoleum. Here
A clutter of Bible and weeping willows guards
The stern Colonial magistrates and wards
Of Charles the Second, and the clouds
Weep on the just and unjust as they will,—
For the poor dead cannot see Easter crowds
On Boston Common or the Beacon Hill
Where strangers hold the golden Statehouse dome
For good and always. Where they live is home:
A common with an iron railing: here
Frayed cables wreathe the spreading cenotaph
Of John and Mary Winslow and the laugh
Of Death is hacked in sandstone, in their year.

A green train grinds along its buried tracks
And screeches. When the great mutation racks
The Pilgrim Fathers' relics, will these placques
Harness the spare-ribbed persons of the dead
To battle with the dragon? Philip's head
Grins on the platter, fouls in pantomime
The fingers of kept time:
"Surely, this people is but grass,"
He whispers, "this will pass;
But, Sirs, the trollop dances on your skulls
And breaks the hollow noddle like an egg
That thought the world an eggshell. Sirs, the gulls
Scream from the squelching wharf-piles, beg a leg
To crack their crops. The Judgment is at hand;
Only the dead are poorer in this world
Where State and elders thundered *raca,* hurled
Anathemas at nature and the land
That fed the hunter's gashed and green perfection—
Its settled mass concedes no outlets for your puns
And verbal Paradises. Your election,
Hawking above this slime
For souls as single as their skeletons,
Flutters and claws in the dead hand of time."

When you go down this man-hole to the drains,
The doorman barricades you in and out;
You wait upon his pleasure. All about
The pale, sand-colored, treeless chains
Of T-squared buildings strain
To curb the spreading of the braced terrain;
When you go down this hole, perhaps your pains
Will be rewarded well; no rough-cast house
Will bed and board you in King's Chapel. Here
A public servant putters with a knife
And paints the railing red
Forever, as a mouse
Cracks walnuts by the headstones of the dead
Whose chiselled angels peer
At you, as if their art were long as life.

I ponder on the railing at this park:
Who was the man who sowed the dragon's teeth,
That fabulous or fancied patriarch
Who sowed so ill for his descent, beneath
King's Chapel in this underworld and dark?
John, Matthew, Luke and Mark,
Gospel me to the Garden, let me come
Where Mary twists the warlock with her flowers—
Her soul a bridal chamber fresh with flowers
And her whole body an ecstatic womb,
As through the trellis peers the sudden Bridegroom.

Mr. Edwards and the Spider

I saw the spiders marching through the air,
Swimming from tree to tree that mildewed day
   In latter August when the hay
    Came creaking to the barn. But where
      The wind is westerly,
Where gnarled November makes the spiders fly
Into the apparitions of the sky,
They purpose nothing but their ease and die
Urgently beating east to sunrise and the sea;

What are we in the hands of the great God?
It was in vain you set up thorn and briar
   In battle array against the fire
    And treason crackling in your blood;
      For the wild thorns grow tame
And will do nothing to oppose the flame;
Your lacerations tell the losing game
You play against a sickness past your cure.
How will the hands be strong? How will the heart endure?

A very little thing, a little worm,
Or hourglass-blazoned spider, it is said,
   Can kill a tiger. Will the dead
    Hold up his mirror and affirm
      To the four winds the smell
And flash of his authority? It's well
If God who holds you to the pit of hell,
Much as one holds a spider, will destroy,
Baffle and dissipate your soul. As a small boy

On Windsor Marsh, I saw the spider die
When thrown into the bowels of fierce fire:
   There's no long struggle, no desire
   To get up on its feet and fly—
     It stretches out its feet
And dies. This is the sinner's last retreat;
Yes, and no strength exerted on the heat
Then sinews the abolished will, when sick
And full of burning, it will whistle on a brick.

   But who can plumb the sinking of that soul?
   Josiah Hawley, picture yourself cast
    Into a brick-kiln where the blast
    Fans your quick vitals to a coal—
     If measured by a glass,
   How long would it seem burning! Let there pass
A minute, ten, ten trillion; but the blaze
Is infinite, eternal: this is death,
To die and know it. This is the Black Widow, death.

After the Surprising Conversions

September twenty-second, Sir: today
I answer. In the latter part of May,
Hard on our Lord's Ascension, it began
To be more sensible. A gentleman
Of more than common understanding, strict
In morals, pious in behavior, kicked
Against our goad. A man of some renown,
An useful, honored person in the town,
He came of melancholy parents; prone
To secret spells, for years they kept alone—
His uncle, I believe, was killed of it:
Good people, but of too much or little wit.
I preached one Sabbath on a text from Kings;
He showed concernment for his soul. Some things
In his experience were hopeful. He
Would sit and watch the wind knocking a tree
And praise this countryside our Lord has made.
Once when a poor man's heifer died, he laid
A shilling on the doorsill; though a thirst
For loving shook him like a snake, he durst
Not entertain much hope of his estate
In heaven. Once we saw him sitting late
Behind his attic window by a light
That guttered on his Bible; through that night
He meditated terror, and he seemed
Beyond advice or reason, for he dreamed
That he was called to trumpet Judgment Day
To Concord. In the latter part of May
He cut his throat. And though the coroner
Judged him delirious, soon a noisome stir

Palsied our village. At Jehovah's nod
Satan seemed more let loose amongst us: God
Abandoned us to Satan, and he pressed
Us hard, until we thought we could not rest
Till we had done with life. Content was gone.
All the good work was quashed. We were undone.
The breath of God had carried out a planned
And sensible withdrawal from this land;
The multitude, once unconcerned with doubt,
Once neither callous, curious nor devout,
Jumped at broad noon, as though some peddler groaned
At it in its familiar twang: "My friend,
Cut your own throat. Cut your own throat. Now! Now!"
September twenty-second, Sir, the bough
Cracks with the unpicked apples, and at dawn
The small-mouth bass breaks water, gorged with spawn.

The Slough of Despond

At sunset only swamp
Afforded pursey tufts of grass . . . these gave,
I sank. Each humus-sallowed pool
Rattled its cynic's lamp
And croaked: "We lay Apollo in his grave;
Narcissus is our fool."

My God, it was a slow
And brutal push! At last I struck the tree
Whose dead and purple arms, entwined
With sterile thorns, said: "Go!
Pluck me up by the roots and shoulder me;
The watchman's eyes are blind."

My arms swung like an axe.
And with my tingling sword I lopped the knot:
The labyrinthine East was mine
But for the asking. Lax
And limp, the creepers caught me by the foot,
And then I toed their line;

I walk upon the flood:
My way is wayward; there is no way out:
Now how the weary waters swell,—
The tree is down in blood!
All the bats of Babel flap about
The rising sun of hell.

The Blind Leading the Blind

NOTHING will hustle: at his own sweet time
My father and his before him humanized
The seedy fields and heaped them on my house
Of straw; no flaring, hurtling thing surprised
Us out of season, and the corn-fed mouse
Reined in his bestial passions. Hildesheim
Survived the passing angel; who'd require
Our passion for the Easter? Satan snored
By the brass railing, while his back-log roared
And coiled its vapors on St. Gertrude's blue stone spire:

A land of mattocks; here the brothers strode,
Hulking as horses in their worsted hose
And cloaks and shin-guards—each had hooked his hoe
Upon his fellow's shoulder; by each nose
The aimless waterlines of eyeballs show
Their greenness. They are blind—blind to the road
And to its Maker. Here my father saw
The leadman trip against a pigpen, crash,
Legs spread, his codpiece split, his fiddle smash . . .
These mammoth vintners danced their blood out in the straw.

The Fens

(AFTER COBBETT)

From Crowland to St. Edmund's to Ipswich
The fens are level as a drawing-board:
Great bowling greens divided by a ditch—
The grass as thick as grows on ground. The Lord
High Sheriff settles here, as on a sea,
When the parochial calm of sunset chills
The world to its four corners. And the hills
Are green with hops and harvest, and a bitch
Spuddles about a vineyard on a tree;

Here everything grows well. Here the fat land
Has no stone bigger than a ladybug,
No milkweed or wild onion can withstand
The sheriff's men, and sunlight sweats the slug.
Here the rack-renting system has its say:
At nightfall sheep as fat as hogs shall lie
Heaped on the mast and corncobs of the sty
And they will rise and take the landlord's hand;
The bailiff bears the Bell, the Bell, away.

The Death of the Sheriff

"forsitan et Priami fuerint quae fata, requiras?"

I

NOLI ME TANGERE

We PARK and stare. A full sky of the stars
Wheels from the pumpkin setting of the moon
And sparks the windows of the yellow farm
Where the red-flannelled madmen look through bars
At windmills thrashing snowflakes by an arm
Of the Atlantic. Soon
The undertaker who collects antiques
Will let his motor idle at the door
And set his pine-box on the parlor floor.
Our homicidal sheriff howled for weeks;

We kiss. The State had reasons: on the whole,
It acted out of kindness when it locked
Its servant in this place and had him watched
Until an ordered darkness left his soul
A *tabula rasa;* when the Angel knocked
The sheriff laid his notched
Revolver on the table for the guest.
Night draws us closer in its bearskin wrap
And our loved sightless smother feels the tap
Of the blind stars descending to the west

65

To lay the Devil in the pit our hands
Are draining like a windmill. Who'll atone
For the unsearchable quicksilver heart
Where spiders stare their eyes out at their own
Spitting and knotted likeness? We must start:
Our aunt, his mother, stands
Singing *O Rock of Ages,* as the light
Wanderers show a man with a white cane
Who comes to take the coffin in his wain,
The thirsty Dipper on the arc of night.

II

THE PORTRAIT

The whiskey circulates, until I smash
The candelabrum from the mantel's top,
And scorch Poseidon on the panel where
He forks the blocks of Troy into the air.
A chipmunk shucks the strychnine in a cup;
The popping pine-cones flash
Like shore-bait on his face in oils. My bile
Rises, and beads of perspiration swell
To flies and splash the *Parmachenie Belle*
That I am scraping with my uncle's file.

I try the barb upon a pencilled line
Of Vergil. Nothing underneath the sun
Has bettered, Uncle, since the scaffolds flamed
On butchered Troy until Aeneas shamed
White Helen on her hams by Vesta's shrine . . .
All that the Greeks have won
I'll cancel with a sidestroke of my sword;
Now I can let my father, wife and son
Banquet Apollo for Laomedon:
Helen will satiate the fire, my Lord.

I search the starlight . . . Helen will appear,
Pura per noctem in luce . . . I am chilled,
I drop the barbless fly into my purse
Beside his nickel shield. It is God's curse,
God's, that has purpled Lucifer with fear
And burning. God has willed;
I lift the window. Digging has begun,
The hill road sparkles, and the mourners' cars
Wheel with the whited sepulchres of stars
To light the worldly dead-march of the sun.

The Dead in Europe

AFTER the planes unloaded, we fell down
Buried together, unmarried men and women;
Not crown of thorns, not iron, not Lombard crown,
Not grilled and spindle spires pointing to heaven
Could save us. Raise us, Mother, we fell down
Here hugger-mugger in the jellied fire:
Our sacred earth in our day was our curse.

Our Mother, shall we rise on Mary's day
In Maryland, wherever corpses married
Under the rubble, bundled together? Pray
For us whom the blockbusters marred and buried;
When Satan scatters us on Rising-day,
O Mother, snatch our bodies from the fire:
Our sacred earth in our day was our curse.

Mother, my bones are trembling and I hear
The earth's reverberations and the trumpet
Bleating into my shambles. Shall I bear,
(O Mary!) unmarried man and powder-puppet,
Witness to the Devil? Mary, hear,
O Mary, marry earth, sea, air and fire;
Our sacred earth in our day is our curse.

Where the Rainbow Ends

I saw the sky descending, black and white,
Not blue, on Boston where the winters wore
The skulls to jack-o'-lanterns on the slates,
And Hunger's skin-and-bone retrievers tore
The chickadee and shrike. The thorn tree waits
Its victim and tonight
The worms will eat the deadwood to the foot
Of Ararat: the scythers, Time and Death,
Helmed locusts, move upon the tree of breath;
The wild ingrafted olive and the root

Are withered, and a winter drifts to where
The Pepperpot, ironic rainbow, spans
Charles River and its scales of scorched-earth miles.
I saw my city in the Scales, the pans
Of judgment rising and descending. Piles
Of dead leaves char the air—
And I am a red arrow on this graph
Of Revelations. Every dove is sold
The Chapel's sharp-shinned eagle shifts its hold
On serpent-Time, the rainbow's epitaph.

In Boston serpents whistle at the cold.
The victim climbs the altar steps and sings:
"Hosannah to the lion, lamb, and beast
Who fans the furnace-face of IS with wings:
I breathe the ether of my marriage feast."
At the high altar, gold
And a fair cloth. I kneel and the wings beat
My cheek. What can the dove of Jesus give
You now but wisdom, exile? Stand and live,
The dove has brought an olive branch to eat.

69